PUFFIN BOOKS

HIP-HOP NATURE BOY

Born in Kasauli in 1934, Ruskin Bond grew up in Jamnagar, Dehradun, New Delhi and Simla. His first novel, *The Room on the Roof*, written when he was seventeen, received the John Llewellyn Rhys Memorial Prize in 1957. Since then he has written over five hundred short stories, essays and novellas (some included in the collections *Dust on the Mountain* and *Classic Ruskin Bond*) and more than forty books for children.

He received the Sahitya Akademi Award for English writing in India in 1993, the Padma Shri in 1999 and the Delhi government's Lifetime Achievement Award in 2012. He was awarded the Sahitya Akademi's Bal Sahitya Puraskar for his 'total contribution to children's literature' in 2013 and was honoured with the Padma Bhushan in 2014. He lives in Landour, Mussoorie, with his extended family.

D1529524

Also in Puffin by Ruskin Bond

Getting Granny's Glasses
Earthquake
The Cherry Tree
The Eyes of the Eagle
Dust on the Mountain
Cricket for the Crocodile
Puffin Classics: The Room on the Roof
Puffin Classics: Vagrants in the Valley
The Room of Many Colours: A Treasury of Stories for Children
Panther's Moon and Other Stories
The Hidden Pool
The Parrot Who Wouldn't Talk and Other Stories
Mr Oliver's Diary
Escape from Java and Other Tales of Danger
Crazy Times with Uncle Ken
Rusty: The Boy from the Hills
Rusty Runs Away
Rusty and the Leopard
Rusty Goes to London
Rusty Comes Home
Rusty and the Magic Mountain
The Puffin Book of Classic School Stories
The Puffin Good Reading Guide for Children
The Kashmiri Storyteller
The Adventures of Rusty: Collected Stories
Thick as Thieves: Tales of Friendship
Uncles, Aunts and Elephants: Tales from Your Favourite Storyteller
Ranji's Wonderful Bat and Other Stories
Whispers in the Dark: A Book of Spooks
The Tree Lover
The Day Grandfather Tickled a Tiger

Hip-Hop Nature Boy
and other poems

RUSKIN BOND

Illustrations by Joy Gosney

PUFFIN BOOKS
An imprint of Penguin Random House

PUFFIN BOOKS

USA | Canada | UK | Ireland | Australia
New Zealand | India | South Africa | China

Penguin Books is part of the Penguin Random House group of companies
whose addresses can be found at global.penguinrandomhouse.com

Published by Penguin Random House India Pvt. Ltd
7th Floor, Infinity Tower C, DLF Cyber City,
Gurgaon 122 002, Haryana, India

First published in Puffin Books by Penguin Books India 2012

ISBN 9780143332121

Typeset in Weiss by InoSoft Systems, Noida
Printed at Replika Press Pvt. Ltd, India

For
Siddharth,
who listened patiently while
I read these poems to him,
and laughed in all the right places.

Contents

Introduction

Nearly all my life I have been writing stories and novels, but now and then I burst into song—that is, I write a poem.

This usually happens when I am feeling very happy, although it can also happen when I am feeling rather morose or melancholy. So, most of my poems have been happy poems. But there have been a few sad ones too.

Sometimes I feel like singing. But I'm an out-of-tune singer; I can never hit the right note. People who are near me don't like to hear me singing, because odd things happen. If I'm in a car, singing, it goes off the road. Birds fall silent. Cows and other animals make a dash for safety. Schoolteachers go into shock. People do everything they can to prevent me from singing.

So now, when I feel like singing, I write a poem. I put my song down on paper, and dance a little jig in my room. Like that, no one can stop me.

My poems are silent songs. I make them up in my head, but they come from the heart.

These poems were written at different periods during my long writing life, although the title poem and a few others were written especially for this collection. Sohini, my Puffin editor (she's actually a girl, not a puffin), selected poems that we thought would appeal to young readers.

I like the funny ones best. But we have mixed them all up, which means you can open the book anywhere and see if you can find something that you like. You can even read the book backwards. In a book of poems it makes no difference.

Ruskin Bond
Landour, Bangalore,
Puri, Mussoorie

(I started this introduction at the beginning of a journey, and finished it when I was back home in Mussoorie.)

Hip-Hop Nature Boy

When I was seven,
And climbing trees,
I stepped into a hive of bees.
Badly stung and mad with pain,
I danced the hip-hop in the rain.
Hip-hop, I'm a nature boy,
Mother Nature's pride and joy!

When I was twelve,
Still climbing trees,
I fell instead—
And landed on my head.
Feeling lighter,
I thought I might become a writer.
Hip-hop, dancing in the rain,
A nature-writer I became!

With Nature being my natural bent,
At twenty I took out my tent,
And spent the night beside a Nadi,
Wearing only vest and chuddee.
At crack of drawn I woke to find
A crocodile was close behind,
And smiling broadly!

In times of crises at my best,
I did not trouble to get dressed,
But fled towards the Gulf of Kutch,
With fond salaams to muggermuch!
Mother Nature once again
Found me dancing on the plain,
Nanga-panga in the rain!

Growing older, even bolder,
Took a winding mountain trail,
Up a hill and down a dale,
All to see a mountain-quail.

The quail was extinct, long expired,
I was limping, very tired;

Thought I saw a comfy cot
In the corner of a hut.
Feeling grateful, I sank down
Upon a blanket soft as down.
Blanket rose up all at once,
Gave a shudder, then a pounce.
Stumbling in the darkness there,
I'd disturbed a big brown bear!

I did not stop to say goodnight,
But fled into the open night.
Hip-hop in the rain,
Dancing to that old refrain.

Growing old, I thought it safer
In my tryst with Mother Nature,
To grow flowers—
Roses, dahlias,
Poppies, sweet peas, rare azaleas,
Candy tuft and tiny tansies,
Violets sweet and naughty pansies . . .
A lovely garden I'd constructed,
Birds and bees were soon inducted.

Bees! Did I say bees?
They were buzzing all around me—
Angry, diving down upon me;
For where their hive had been suspended,
By accident it lay upended!

Dear Reader, if you must
In Nature put your trust,
Stay away from swarms of bees
And strange crocs lurking under trees,
Or else, like me, you'll dance with pain
While doing the hip-hop in the rain.

Look for the Colours of Life

Colours are everywhere,
Bright blue the sky,
Dark green the forest
And light the fresh grass;
Bright yellow the lights
From a train sweeping past,
The Flame trees glow
At this time of year,
The mangoes burn bright
As the monsoon draws near.

A favourite colour of mine
Is the pink of the candyfloss man
As he comes down the dusty road,
Calling his wares;
And the balloon-man soon follows,
Selling his floating bright colours.

It's early summer
And the roses blush
In the dew-drenched dawn,
And poppies sway red and white
In the invisible breeze.
Only the wind has no colour:

But if you look carefully
You will see it teasing
The colour out of the leaves.
And the rain has no colour
But it turns the bronzed grass
To emerald green,
And gives a golden sheen
To the drenched sunflower.
Look for the colours of life—
They are everywhere,
Even in your dreams.

All is Life

Whether by accident or design,
We are here.
Let's make the most of it, my friend.
Make happiness our pursuit,
Spread a little sunshine here and there.
Enjoy the flowers, the breeze,
Rivers, sea, and sky,
Mountains and tall waving trees.
Greet the children passing by,
Talk to the old folk. Be kind, my friend.
Hold on, in times of pain and strife:
Until death comes, all is life.

A Plea for Bowlers

Cricket never will be fair
Till bowlers get their rightful share
For toiling in the midday sun.
What should be done?
It's simple—
Make those wickets broader, taller!
That should make it much more fun
For the poor perspiring bowler.

P.S. And in the interests of the game
 The size of the bat remains the same.

To Live in Magic

What more perfect friend
than the friend you have given me, Lord;
What more perfect song than the
whistling-thrush at dawn's first light;
What lovelier thing than the ladybird
opening its wings on the rose-petal;
What greater gift than this moment in time,
this heartbeat in the night?

We Must Love Someone

We must love someone
If we are to justify
Our presence on this earth.
We must keep loving all our days,
Someone, anyone, anywhere
Outside our selves;
For even the sarus crane
Will grieve over its lost companion,
And the seal its mate.
Somewhere in life
There must be someone
To take your hand
And share the torrid day.
Without the touch of love
There is no life, and we must fade away.

This Land is Mine

This land is mine
Although I do not own it,
This land is mine
Because I grew upon it.
This dust, this grass,
This tender leaf
And weathered bark
All in my heart are finely blended
Until my time on earth is ended.

Raindrop

This leaf, so complete in itself,
Is only part of a tree.
And this tree, so complete in itself,
Is only part of the mountain.
And the mountain runs down to the sea.
And the sea, so complete in itself,
Rests like a raindrop
On the hand of God.

Love's Sad Song

There's a sweet little girl lives down the lane,
And she's so pretty and I'm so plain,
She's clever and smart and all things good,
And I'm the bad boy of the neighbourhood.
But I'd be her best friend forever and a day
If only she'd smile and look my way.

A Little Night Music

Open the window
Let in the Night
All that is lovely
Comes at this hour
Moonlight and moonbeam
And fragrance of flower
Blossoming Champa
And Queen of the Night—
And sometimes a field mouse
Drops in for a bite.
High in the treetops
An owl strikes a note
And the frogs in their pond
Sing out as they float
Along on their lily pads . . .
The brainfever bird

Is calling on high
'Brain fever, brain fever!'—
Its monotonous cry.
The nightjar plays trombone
The crickets join in
An out-of-tune orchestra
Making a din!
I lie awake listening
To the wild duck in flight
As they fly to the north
For their annual respite;
And a star in the heavens
Sweeps past as it falls,
A leopard's out hunting—
The swamp deer calls.
A breeze has sprung up,
It hums in the trees
The window is rattling
And I must cease
From my Nocturne
And shut out the Night.

Goodnight, birds
Goodnight, frogs
Goodnight, stars
Goodnight sweet Night.

The Demon Driver

At driving a car I've never been good—
I batter the bumper and damage the hood—
'Get off the road!' the traffic cops shout,
'You're supposed to go *round* that roundabout!'
'I thought it was quicker to drive straight
through.'
'Give us your license — it's time to renew.'
I took their advice and handed a fee
To a Babu who looked on this windfall with glee.
'No problem,' he said, 'Your license now pukka,
You may drive all the way from here to Kolkata.'

So away I drove, at a feverish pitch,
Advancing someway down an unseen ditch.
Once back on the highway, I soon joined the
fray

Of hundreds of drivers who wouldn't give way:
I skimmed past a truck and revolved round a van
(Good drivers can do anything that they can)
Then offered a lift to a man with a load—
'Just a little way down to the end of this road.'
As I pressed on the pedal, the car gave a
shudder:
He'd got in at one door, got out at the other.
'God help you!' he said, as he hurried away,
'I'll come for a drive another fine day!'
I came to that roundabout, round it I sped
Eager to get to my dinner and bed.
Round it I went, and round it once more
'Get off the road!' That cop was a bore.
I swung to the left and went clean through a
wall,
My neighbour stood there—he looked
menacing, tall—
'This will cost you three thousand,' he quietly
said,
'And send me your cheque before you're in bed!'

Alas! my new car was sent for repair,
But my friends gathered round and said, never despair!
'We are all going to help you to make a fresh start.'
And next day they gave me a nice bullock-cart.

Summer Fruit

Summer is here, and mangoes too
And fruit of every taste and hue;
And given a choice of juice or berry,
I'll settle for the humble cherry.
I know *your* favourite on this planet
Is the red and rosy pomegranate;
But that's a winter fruit, my child,
So wait until the weather's mild.
But if you like a simple khana,
There's nothing like a good banana.
No? Something more exotic?
Maybe some lichis in your pockets.
Or would you like a large tarbuj—
It's sweeter than a good kharbuj—
Tarbuj, kharbuja — oh, what's the difference?
Tell me, children, and your preference.

Dandelion

I think it's an insult
To Nature's generosity
That many call this cheerful flower
A 'common weed'.
How dare they so degrade
A flower divinely made!
Sublimely does it bloom and seed
In sunshine or in shade,
Thriving in wind and rain,
On stony soil
On walls or steps
On strips of waste;
Tough and resilient,
Giving delight
When other flowers are out of sight.

And when its puff-ball comes to fruit
You make a wish and blow it clean away:

'Please make my wish come true,' you say.
And if you're kind and pure of heart,
Who knows? This magic flower might just
respond
And help you on your way.
Good dandelion,
Be mine today.

Love is a Law

Who shall set a law to lovers?
Love is a law unto itself

Love gained is often lost
And love that's lost is found again

It's love that makes the world go round
Love that keeps us closely bound

Take this power to love away
We would be just beasts of prey

If Love should lose its hold on us
Discord would rule the Universe.

Firefly in My Room

Last night, as I lay sleepless
In the summer dark
With window open to invite a breeze,
Softly a firefly flew in
And circled round the room
Twinkling at me from floor or wall
Or ceiling, never long in one place
But lighting up little spaces . . .
A friendly presence, dispelling
The settled gloom of an unhappy day.

And after it had gone, I left
The window open, just in case
It should return.

Rain

After weeks of heat and dust
How welcome is the rain.
It washes the leaves,
Gives new life to grass,
Draws out the scent of the earth.
It rattles on the roof,
Gurgles along the drainpipe
Collects in a puddle in the middle of the lawn—
The birds come to bathe.

When the sun comes out
A lizard crawls up from a crack in a rock.
'Small brown lizard
Basking in the sun
You too have your life to live
Your race to run.'

At night we look through the branches
Of the cherry tree.
The sky is rainwashed, star-bright.

If Mice Could Roar

If mice could roar
And elephants soar,
And trees grow up in the sky;
If tigers could dine
On biscuits and wine,
And the fattest of men could fly!
If pebbles could sing
and bells never ring
And teachers were lost in the post;
If a tortoise could run
And losses be won,
And bullies be buttered on toast;
If a song brought a shower
And a gun grew a flower,
This world would be nicer than most!

So Beautiful the Night

I love the night, Lord.
After the sun's heat and the day's work,
It's good to close my eyes and rest my body.
It's a good time for small creatures:
Porcupines come out of their burrows
to dig for roots.
The nightjar calls tonk-tonk!
The timid owl peeps out of his hole in the tree
trunk
Where he has been hiding all day.
Insects crawl out in thousands.
The wind comes down the chimney
and blows around the room.
I'm watching the stars from my window.
The trees are stretching their arms in the dark
and whispering to the moon.

But if the trees could walk, Lord,
What a wonderful sight it would be—
Armies of pines and firs and oaks
Marching over the moonlit mountains.

What Can We Give Our Children?

What can we give our children?
Knowledge, yes, and honour too,
And strength of character
And the gift of laughter.
What gold do we give our children?
The gold of a sunny childhood,
Open spaces, a home that binds
Us to the common good . . .
These simple things
Are greater than the gold of kings.

A Frog Screams

Standing near a mountain stream
I heard a sound like the creaking
Of a branch in the wind.
It was a frog screaming
In the jaws of a long green snake.

I couldn't bear that hideous cry.
And taking two sharp sticks,
I made the twisting snake disgorge the frog,
Who hopped quite spry out of the snake's mouth
And sailed away on a floating log.

Pleased with the outcome,
I released the green grass-snake,
Stood back and spoke aloud:
'Is this what it feels like to be God?'

'Only what it's like to be English,'
Said God (speaking for a change in French);
'I would have let the snake finish his lunch!'

The Cat Has Something to Say

Sir, you're a human and I'm a cat,
And I'm really quite happy to leave it at that.
It doesn't concern me if you like a dish
Of chicken masala or lobster and fish.
So why all these protests around the house
If for dinner I fancy
A succulent mouse?
Or a careless young sparrow who came my way?
Our natures, dear sir, are really the same:
Flesh, fish or fowl, we both like our game.
Only you take yours curried,
And I take mine plain.

Lone Fox Dancing

As I walked home last night
I saw a lone fox dancing
In the cold moonlight.

I stood and watched. Then
Took the low road, knowing
The night was his by right.

Sometimes, when words ring true,
I'm like a lone fox dancing
In the morning dew.

Self-Portrait

There was an old man in Landour
Who wanted young folk to laugh more;
So he wrote them a book,
And with laughter they shook
As they rolled down the hill to Rajpore.

Granny's Tree-Climbing

My grandmother was a genius. You'd like to
know why?
Because she could climb trees. Spreading or
high,
She'd be up their branches in a trice. And mind
you,
When last she climbed a tree, she was sixty-two.
Ever since childhood, she'd had this gift
For being happier in a tree than in a lift;
And though, as years went by, she would be told
That climbing trees should stop when one grew
old
And that growing old should be gone about
gracefully
She'd laugh and say, 'Well, I'll grow old
disgracefully.
I can do it better.' And we had to agree;

For in all the garden there wasn't a tree
She hadn't been up, at one time or another
(Having learned to climb from a loving brother
When she was six) but it was feared by all
That one day she'd have a terrible fall.
The outcome was different; while we were in
town
She climbed a tree and couldn't come down!

We went to the rescue, and helped her descend . . .
A doctor took Granny's temperature and said,
'I strongly recommend a quiet week in bed.'
We sighed with relief and tucked her up well.
Poor Granny! For her, it was more like a season
in hell.

Confined to her bedroom, while every breeze
Whispered of summer and dancing leaves.
But she held her peace till she felt stronger
Then sat up and said, 'I'll lie here no longer!'
And she called for my father and told him
undaunted
That a house in a treetop was what she now
wanted.

My dad knew his duties. He said, 'That's all right
You'll have what you want, dear, I'll start work tonight.'
With my expert assistance, he soon finished the chore:
Made her a tree house with windows and a door.
So Granny moved up, and now every day
I climb to her room with glasses and a tray.
She sits there in state and drinks mocktails with me,
Upholding her right to reside in a tree.

Do You Believe in Ghosts?

'Do you believe in ghosts?'
Asked the passenger
On platform number three.
'I'm a rational man,' said I,
'I believe in what I can see—
Your hands, your feet, your beard!'
'Then look again,' said he,
And promptly disappeared!

Portents

Spider running up the wall
Means that rain is going to fall.

Spider running down the wall
Means the house is going to fall!

In Praise of the Sausage

I like a good sausage, I do;
It's a dish for the chosen and few.
Oh, for sausage and mash,
And of mustard a dash,
And an egg nicely fried—maybe two?
At breakfast or lunch, or at dinner,
The sausage is always a winner;
If you want a good spread
Go for sausage on bread,
And forget all your vows to be slimmer.

Don't Be Afraid of the Dark

Don't be afraid of the dark, little one,
The earth must rest when the day is done.
The sun may be harsh, but moonlight—never!
And those stars will be shining forever and ever,
Be friends with the Night, there is nothing to
fear,
Just let your thoughts travel to friends far and
near.
By day, it does seem that our troubles won't
cease,
But at night, late at night, the world is at peace.

Walk Tall

You stride through the long grass,
Pressing on over fallen pine-needles,
Up the winding road to the mountain pass:
Small red ant, now crossing a sea
Of raindrops; your destiny
To carry home that single, slender
Cosmos seed,
Waving it like a banner in the sun.

Silent Birth

When the earth gave birth to this tree,
There came no sound:
A green shoot thrust
In silence from the ground.
Our births don't come so quiet—
Most lives run riot—
But the bud opens silently,
And flower gives way to fruit.
So must we search
For the stillness within the tree,
The silence within the root.

Listen!

Listen to the night wind in the trees,
Listen to the summer grass singing;
Listen to the time that's tripping by,
And the dawn dew falling.
Listen to the moon as it climbs the sky,
Listen to the pebbles humming;
Listen to the mist in the trembling leaves,
And the silence calling.

Cherry Tree

Eight years have passed
Since I placed my cherry seed in the grass.
'Must have a tree of my own,' I said—
And watered it once and went to bed
And forgot; but cherries have a way of growing
Though no one's caring very much or knowing,
And suddenly that summer, near the end of May,
I found a tree had come to stay.
It was very small, a five months' child,
Lost in the tall grass running wild.
Goats ate the leaves, a grasscutter's scythe
Split it apart, and a monsoon blight
Shrivelled the slender stem . . . Even so,
Next spring I watched three new shoots grow,
The young tree struggle, upwards thrust
Its arms in a fresh fierce lust
For light and air and sun.

I could only wait, as one
Who watches, wondering, while Time and the
rain
Made a miracle from green, growing pain . . .
I went away next year—
Spent a season in Kashmir—
Came back thinner, rather poor,
But richer by a cherry tree at my door.
Six feet high, my own dark cherry,
And—I could scarcely believe it—a berry,
Ripened and jewelled in the sun,
Hung from a branch—just one!
And next year there were blossoms, small
Pink, fragile, quick to fall
At the merest breath, the sleepiest breeze . . .

I lay on the grass, at ease,
Looked up through leaves, at the blue
Blind sky, at the finches as they flew
And flitted through the dappled green,
While bees in an ecstasy drank
Of nectar from each bloom, and the sun sank

Swiftly, and the stars turned in the sky,
And moon-moths and singing crickets and I—
Yes, I!—praised night and stars and tree:
A small, tall cherry grown by me.

View from the Window

I'm in bed with fever
But the fever's not high.
Beside my bed is a window
And I like looking out at all
That's happening around me.
The cherry leaves are turning a dark green.
On the maple tree, winged seeds spin round and
round.
There is fruit on the wild blackberry bushes.
Two mynah birds are building a nest in a hole—
They are very noisy about it.
Bits of grass keep falling on the window sill.
High up in the spruce tree, a hawk-cuckoo calls:
'I slept so well, I slept so well!'
When the hawk-cuckoo is awake, no one else
sleeps,

That's why it's also known as the fever bird.
A small squirrel climbs on the window sill.
He's been coming every day since I've been ill,
and I give him crumbs from my tray.
A boy on a mule passes by on the rough
mountain track.
He sees my face at the window and waves to me.
I wave back to him.
When I'm better I'll ask him to let me ride his
mule.

Boy in a Blue Pullover

Boy in a faded blue pullover,
Poor boy, thin, smiling boy,
Ran down the road shouting,
Singing, flinging his arms wide.
I stood in the way and stopped him.
'What's up?' I said. 'Why are you happy?'
He showed me the nickel rupee-coin.
'I found it on the road,' he said.
And he held it to the light
That he might see it shining bright.
'And how will you spend it,
Small boy in blue pullover?'
'I'll buy—
I'll buy a buckle for my belt!'
Slim boy, smart boy,
Would buy a buckle for his belt

Coin clutched in his hot hand,
He ran off laughing, bright.
The coin I'd lost an hour ago;
But better his that night.

Little One Don't Be Afraid

Little one, don't be afraid of this big river.
Be safe in these warm arms for ever.
Grow tall, my child, be wise and strong.
But do not take from any man his song.
Little one, don't be afraid of this dark night.
Walk boldly as you see the truth and light.
Love well, my child, laugh all day long,
But do not take from any man his song.

October

October comes . . .
The mountains resonate
To festive drums.
At sunset time
The western sky
Is drenched
A crimson winterline.
October's here.
The pilgrims come
Steep hills to climb,
For now
It's Durga-puja time.

At Ganga's mouth
The icy waters
Issue forth.

The hills resound
As waters from the north
Sweep down . . .
The mighty river
Makes its way
And winds along
To Bangla's Bay.

The days speed by,
Diwali lamps
Are shining forth
From East and West
And South and North.
The goddess smiles,
Our heads bow down,
We pray
For better things to come.

October's gone!
The night's grow long,
We sing a softer
Sadder song,

Recalling hopes of yesterday,
Lost loves, lost dreams . . .
But still we pray
For better times to come our way.

The Owl

At night, when all is still,
The forest's sentinel
Glides silently across the hill
And perches in an old pine tree.
A friendly presence his!
No harm can come
From night bird on the prowl.
His cry is mellow,
Much softer than a peacock's call.
Why then this fear of owls
Calling in the night?
If men must speak,
Then owls must hoot—
They have the right.

On me it casts no spell:
Rather, it seems to cry,
'The night is good—all's well, all's well.'

The Trees

At seven, when dusk slips over the mountains
The trees start whispering among themselves.
They have been standing still all day.
But now they stretch their limbs in the dark
Shifting a little, flexing their fingers,
Remembering the time when
They too walked the earth with men.
They know me well, these trees:
Oak and walnut, spruce and pine
They know my face in the windows
They know me for a dreamer of dreams
A world-loser, one of them.
They watch me while I watch them grow.
I listen to their whisperings,

Their own mysterious diction;
And bow my head before their arms
And ask for benediction.

Tigers Forever

May there always be tigers, Lord.
In the jungles and tall grass
May the tiger's roar be heard,
May his thunder
Be known in the land.
At the forest pool, by moonlight
May he drink and raise his head
Scenting the night wind.
May he crouch low in the grass
When the herdsmen pass,
And slumber in dark caverns
When the sun is high.
May there always be tigers, Lord.

But not so many that one of them
Might be tempted to come into my bedroom
In search of a meal!

The Snail

Leaving the safety of a rocky ledge
The snail sets out
On his long journey
Across a busy path.
The grass is greener on the other side!
For tender leaf or juicy stem
He'll brave the hazards of the road.
Not made to dodge or weave or run
He must await each threatening step
Chancing his luck
Keeping his tentacles crossed!
Though all unaware
Of the dangers of being squashed
He does not pause or flinch—
A cartwheel misses by an inch!—
But slithers on,
Intent on dinner.

He's there at last, his prize—
Rich leaf-mould where the grass grows tall.
I salute you, Snail.
Somehow, you've made me feel quite small.

The Snake

When, after days of rain,
The sun appears
The snake emerges,
Green-gold on the grass.
Kept in so long,
He basks for hours
Soaks up the hot bright sun.
Knowing how shy he is of me,
I walk a gentle pace
Letting him doze in peace.
But to the snake, earth-bound,
Each step must sound like thunder.
He glides away,
Goes underground.

I've known him for some years:
A harmless green grass-snake
Who, when he sees me on the path,
Uncoils and disappears.

Once You Have Lived with Mountains

Once you have lived with mountains
Under the whispering pines
And deodars, near stars
And a brighter moon,
With wood smoke and mist
Sweet smell of grass, dew lines
On spider-spun, sun-kissed
Buttercup and vine;
Once you have lived with these,
Blessed, God's favourite then,
You will return,
You will come back

To touch the trees and grass
And climb once more the windswept
mountain pass.

Butterfly Time

April showers
Bring swarms of butterflies
Streaming across the valley
Seeking sweet nectar.
Yellow, gold, and burning bright,
Red and blue and banded white.
To my eyes they bring delight!
Theirs a long and arduous flight,
Here today and off tomorrow,
Floating on, bright butterflies,
To distant bowers.
For Nature does things in good order:
And birds and butterflies recognize
No man-made border.

Slum Children at Play

Imps of mischief,
Barefoot in the dust,
Grinning, mocking, even as
They beg you for a crust.
No angels these,
Just hungry eyes
And eager hands
To help you sympathize . . .
They don't want love,
They don't seek pity,
They know there's nothing
In this heartless city
But a kindred need
In those who strive
For power and pelf
Though only just alive!

They know your guilt,
They'll take your money,
And if you give too much
They'll find you funny.
Because that's what you are—
You're just a joke—
Your life is soft
And theirs all grime and smoke.
And yet they shout and sing
And do not thank your giving,
You'll fuss and fret through life
While they do all the living.

The Whistling Schoolboy

From the gorge above Gangotri
Down to Kochi by the sea,
The whistling-thrush keeps singing
That same sweet melody.

He was a whistling schoolboy once,
Who heard god Krishna's flute,
And tried to play the same sweet tune,
But touched a faulty note.

Said Krishna to the errant youth—
A bird you must become,
And you shall whistle all your days
Until your song is done.

For Silence

Thank you, Lord, for silence;
The silence of great mountains
and deserts and forests.
For the silence of the street
late at night
when the last travellers
are safely home
and the traffic is still.
For the silence in my room
in which I can hear small sounds outside:
a moth fluttering against the window pane,
the drip of the dew running off the roof,
and a field mouse rustling through dry leaves.

These Simple Things

The simplest things in life are best—
A patch of green,
A small bird's nest,
A drink of water, fresh and cold,
The taste of bread,
A song of old;
These are the things that matter most.
The laughter of a child,
A favourite book,
Flowers growing wild,
A cricket singing in a shady nook;
A ball that bounces high!
A summer shower,

A rainbow in the sky,
The touch of a loving hand,
And time to rest—
These simple things in life are best.

Granny's Proverbs

A hungry man is an angry man,
 Said dear old Gran
As she prepared an Irish stew
For the chosen few
(Gran'dad, my cousins and me).
But then she'd turn to me and emote—
'Don't be greedy, or your tongue will cut your
throat!'
And if I asked for more of my favourite fish,
'That small fish,' she'd say, 'is better than
an empty dish!'
Like Manu, she taught us to honour our food,
She was the law-giver, seeking all good.
Gran'dad and I, we'd eat what we were given
(Irish stew and a tart)

But sometimes we'd sneak away to the bazaar
To feast on tikkees and chaat
—And that was heaven!

We Are the Babus

Soak the rich and harry the poor,
That's our motto and our law;
We are the rulers of this land,
We are the babus, a merry band,
Under the table, or through the back door,
We'll empty your pockets and ask for more!
We are the babus, this is our law—
Soak the rich and harry the poor!

In a Strange Cafe

Waiter, where's my soup?
On its way, sir, loop the loop!
Straight from our famous cooking pot,
Here it comes, sir, piping hot!

But waiter, there's a fly in my soup.
That's no fly, sir,
That's your chicken.
The smaller the chicken the better the soup!

Please take it away.
I'll just have the curry and a plate of rice . . .
The curry's very good, sir, full of spice!
Waiter, what's this object that's floating around?
Just a small beetle, sir,
Homeward bound!

Never mind the curry, just bring me some bread,
I have to eat something before I'm in bed.
What's on the menu? Hungarian Goulash?
I suppose it's served up with beetles and mash.
Isn't these anything else I can eat?
Yes sir, you could try the crow's feet.
Highly recommended and good for the teeth.

All our best guests
Are most happily fed here.
And where are they now?
All happily dead, sir.

Remember the Old Road

Remember the old road,
The steep stony path
That took us up from Rajpur,
Toiling and sweating
And grumbling at the climb,
But enjoying it all the same.
At first the hills were hot and bare,
But then there were trees near Jharipani
And we stopped at the Halfway House
And swallowed lungfuls of diamond-cut air.
Then onwards, upwards, to the town,
Our appetites to repair!

Well, no one uses the old road any more.
Walking is out of fashion now.
And if you have a car to take you
Swiftly up the motor-road

Why bother to toil up a disused path?
You'd have to be an old romantic like me
To want to take that route again.

But I did it last year,
Pausing and plodding and gasping for air—
Both road and I being a little worse for wear!
But I made it to the top and stopped to rest
And looked down to the valley and the silver
stream
Winding its way towards the plains.
And the land stretched out before me, and the
years fell away,
And I was a boy again,
And the friends of my youth were there beside
me,
And nothing had changed.

A Song for Lost Friends

The past is always with us, for it feeds the
present . . .

I

As a boy I stood on the edge of the railway-
cutting,
Outside the dark tunnel, my hands touching
The hot rails, waiting for them to tremble
At the coming of the noonday train.
The whistle of the engine hung on the forest's
silence.
Then out of the tunnel, a green-gold dragon
Came plunging, thundering past—
Out of the tunnel, out of the grinning dark.

And the train rolled on, every day

Hundreds of people coming or going or running
away—
Goodbye, goodbye!
I haven't seen you again, bright boy at the
carriage window,
Waving to me, calling,
But I've loved you all these years and looked for
you everywhere,
In cities and villages, beside the sea,
In the mountains, in crowds at distant places;

Returning always to the forest's silence,
To watch the windows of some passing train . . .

2

My father took me by the hand and led me
Among the ruins of old forts and palaces.
We lived in a tent near the tomb of Humayun,
Among old trees. Now multi-storeyed blocks
Rise from the plain—tomorrow's ruins . . .
You can explore them, my son, when the trees
Take over again and the thorn-apple grows

In empty windows. There were seven cities
before . . .

Nothing my father said could bring my mother
home;
She had gone with another. He took me to the
hills
In a small train, the engine having palpitations
As it toiled up the steep slopes peopled
With pines and rhododendrons. Through
tunnels
To Simla. Boarding school. He came to see me
In the holidays. We caught butterflies together.
'Next year,' he said, 'when the War is over,
We'll go to England.' But wars are never over
And I have yet to go to England with my father.

He died that year
And I was dispatched to my mother and
stepfather—
A long journey through a dark tunnel.

No one met me at the station. So I wandered
Round Dehra in a tonga, looking for a house
With lichi trees. She'd written to say there were
lichis in the garden.
But in Dehra all the houses had lichi trees,
The tonga-driver charged five rupees
for taking me back to the station.
They were looking for me on the platform:
'We thought the train would be late as usual.'
It had arrived on time, upsetting everyone's
schedule.

In my new home I found a new baby in a new
pram.
Your little brother, they said, which made me a
hundred.
But he too was left behind with the servants
When my mother and Mr H went hunting
Or danced late at the casino, our only wartime
nightclub.
Tommies and Yanks scuffled drunk and
disorderly

In a private war for the favours of stale women.

Lonely in the house with the servants and the
child
And books I'd read twice and my father's letters,
Treasured secretly in the small trunk beneath my
bed:
I wrote to him once but did not post the letter,
For fear it might come back 'Return to
sender . . .'

One day I slipped into the guava orchard next
door—
It really belonged to Seth Hari Kishore
Who'd gone to the Ganga on a pilgrimage—
The guavas were ripe and ready for boys to steal
(Always sweeter when stolen)
And a bare leg thrust at me as I climbed:

'There's only room for one,' came a voice.
I looked up at a boy who had blackberry eyes
And guava juice on his chin, grabbed at him
And we both tumbled out of the tree

On to the ragged December grass. We rolled
and fought
But not for long. A gardener came shouting,
And we broke and ran—over the gate and down
the road
And across the fields and a dry river bed,
Into the shades of afternoon . . .
'Why didn't you run home?' he said.
'Why didn't you?'
'There's no one there, my mother's out.'
'And mine's at home.'

3

His mother was Burmese; his father
An English soldier killed in the War.
They were waiting for it to be over.
Every day, beyond the gardens, we loafed:
Time was suspended for a time.
On heavy wings, ringed pheasants rose
At our approach.
The fields were yellow with mustard,
Parrots wheeled in the sunshine, dipped and
disappeared

Into the morning mist on the foothills.
We found a pool, fed by a freshet
Of cold spring water. 'One day when we are
men,'
He said, 'We'll meet here at the pool again.
Promise?' 'Promise,' I said. And we took a pledge,
In blood, nicking our fingers on a penknife
And pressing them to each other's lips. Sweet,
salty kiss.
Late evening, past cowdust time, we trudged
home:
He to his mother, I to my dinner.

One wining-dancing night I thought I'd stay out
too.
We went to the pictures—*Gone with the Wind*—
A crashing bore for boys, and it finished late.
So I had dinner with them, and his mother said:
'It's past ten. You'd better stay the night.
 But will they miss you?'

I did not answer but climbed into my friend's
bed—

I'd never slept with anyone before, except my
father—
And when it grew cold, after midnight,
He put his arms around me and looped a leg
Over mine and it was nice that way.
But I stayed awake with the niceness of it
My sleep stolen by his own deep slumber . . .
What dreams were lost, I'll never know!
But next morning, just as we'd started breakfast,
A car drew up, and my parents, outraged,
Chastised me for staying out and hustled me
home.
Breakfast unfinished. My friend unhappy. My
pride wounded.
We met sometimes, but a constraint had grown
upon us,
And the following month I heard he'd gone
To an orphanage in Kalimpong.

4

I remember you well, old banyan tree,
As you stood there spreading quietly
Over the broken wall.

While adults slept, I crept away
Down the broad veranda steps, around
The outhouse and the melon-ground . . .
In that winter of long ago, I roamed
The faded garden of my mother's home.

I must have known that giants have few friends
(The great lurk shyly in their private dens),
And found you hidden by a thick green wall
Of aerial roots.
Intruder in your pillared den, I stood
And shyly touched your old and wizened wood,
And as my heart explored you, giant tree,
I heard you singing!

The spirit of the tree became my friend,
Took me to his silent throbbing heart
And taught me the value of stillness.
My first tutor; friend of the lonely.

And the second was the tonga-man
Whose pony-cart came rattling along the road
Under the furthest arch of the banyan tree.

Looking up, he waved his whip at me
And laughing, called, 'Who lives up there?'
'I do,' I said.
And the next time he came along, he stopped
the tonga
And asked me if I felt lonely in the tree.
'Only sometimes,' I said. 'When the tree is
thinking.'
'I never think,' he said. 'You won't feel lonely
with me.'
And with a flick of the reins he rattled away,
With a promise he'd give me a ride someday.
And from him I learnt the value of promises
kept.

5

From the tree to the tonga was an easy drop.
I fell into life. Bansi, tonga-driver,
Wore a yellow waistcoat and spat red
Betel-juice the entire width of the road.
'I can spit further than any man,' he claimed.

It is natural for a man to strive to excel
At something; he spat with authority.

When he took me for rides, he lost a fare.
That was his way. He once said, 'If a girl
Wants five rupees for a fix, bargain like hell
And then give six.'
It was the secret of his failure, he claimed,
To give away more than he owned.
And to prove it, he borrowed my pocket money
In order to buy a present for his mistress.

A man who fails well is better than one who
succeeds badly.

The rattletrap tonga and the winding road
Through the valley, to the riverbed,
With the wind in my hair and the dust
Rising, and the dogs running and barking

And Bansi singing and shouting in my ear,
And the pony farting as it cantered along,

Wheels creaking, seat shifting,
Hood slipping off, the entire contraption
Always about to disintegrate, collapse,
But never quite doing so—like the man
himself . . .
All this was music,
And the ragtime-raga lingers in my mind.

Nostalgia comes swiftly when one is forty,
Looking back at boyhood years.
Even unhappiness acquires a certain glow.

It was shady in the cemetery, and the mango
trees
Did well there, nourished by the bones
Of long-dead Colonels, Collectors, Magistrates
and Memsahibs.
For here, in dusty splendour, lay the graves
Of those who'd brought their English dust
To lie with Ganges soil: some tombs were
temples,
Some were cenotaphs, and one, a tiny Taj.
Here lay sundry relatives, including Uncle

Henry,
Who'd been for many years a missionary.
'Sacred to the Memory
Of Henry C. Wagstaff',
Who translated the Gospels into Pashtu,
And was murdered by his own chowkidar.

'Well done, thou good and faithful servant'—
So ran his epitaph.

The gardener, who looked after the trees,
Also dug graves. One day
I found him working at the bottom of a new
cavity,
'They never let me know in time,' he grumbled.
'Last week I dug two graves, and now, without
warning,
Here's another. It isn't even the season for dying.
There's enough work all summer, when cholera's
about—
Why can't they keep alive through the winter?'
Near the railway lines, watching the trains
(There were six every day, coming or going),

And across the line, the leper colony . . .
I did not know they were lepers till later
But I knew they were different: some
Were without fingers or toes
And one had no nose
And a few had holes in their faces
And yet some were beautiful.
They had their children with them
And the children were no different
From other children.
I made friends with some
And won most of their marbles
And carried them home in my pockets.

One day my parents found me
Playing near the leper colony.
There was a big scene.
My mother shouted at the lepers
And they hung their heads as though it was all
their fault,
And the children had nothing to say.
I was taken home in disgrace
And told all about leprosy and given a bath.

My clothes were thrown away
And the servants wouldn't touch me for days.
So I took the marbles I'd won
And put them in my stepfather's cupboard,
Hoping he'd catch leprosy from them.

6

A slim dark youth with quiet
Eyes and a gentle quizzical smile,
Manohar. Fifteen, working in a small hotel.
He'd come from the hills and wanted to return.
I forget how we met
But I remember walking the dusty roads
With this gentle boy, who held my hand
And told me about his home, his mother,
His village, and the little river
At the bottom of the hill where the water
Ran blue and white and wonderful,
'When I go home, I'll take you with me.'
But we hadn't enough money.
So I sold my bicycle for thirty rupees
And left a note in the dining room:

'Going away. Don't worry—(hoping they
would)—
I'll come home
When I've grown up.'

We crossed the rushing waters of the Ganga
Where they issued from the doors of Vishnu,
Then took the pilgrim road, in those days
Just a stony footpath into the mountains:
Not all who ventured forth returned;
Some came to die, of course,
Near the sacred waters or at their source.
We took this route and spent a night
At a wayside inn, wrapped tight
In the single blanket I'd brought along;
Even then we were cold
It was not the season for pilgrims
And the inn was empty, except for the locals
Drinking a local brew.

We drank a little and listened
To an old soldier from the hills
Talking of the women he'd known

In the first Great War, when stationed in Rome,
His memories were good for many drinks
In many inns, his face pickled in the suns
Of many mountain summers.
The mule-drivers slept in one room
And talked all night over hookahs.
Manohar slept bravely, but I lay watching
A bright star through the tiny window
And wished upon it, already knowing that
wishes
Had no power, but wishing all the same . . .
And next morning we set off again
Leaving the pilgrim route to march
Down a valley, above a smaller river,
Walking until I felt
We'd walk and walk for ever.
Late at night, on a cold mountain,
Two lonely figures, we saw the lights
Of scattered houses and knew we had arrived.

7

'Not death, but a summing-up of life,'
Said the village patriarch, as we watched him

Treasure a patch of winter sunshine
On his string cot in the courtyard.
I remember his wisdom.
And I remember faces.
For it's faces I remember best.
The people were poor, and the patriarch said:
'I have heard it told that the sun
Sets in splendour in Himalaya—
But who can eat sunsets?'

Perhaps, if I'd stayed longer,
I would have yearned for creature comforts.
We were hungry sometimes, eating wild berries
Or slyly milking another's goat,
Or catching small fish in the river . . .
But I did not long for home.
Could I have grown up a village boy,
Grazing sheep and cattle, while the Collected
Works
Of W. Shakespeare lay gathering dust
In Dehra? Who knows? But it was nice

Of my stepfather to send his office manager
Into the mountains to bring me home!

Manohar.
He called goodbye and waved
As I looked back from the bend in the road.
Bright boy on the mountainside,
Waving to me, calling, and I've loved you
All these years and looked for you everywhere,
In the mountains, in crowds at distant places,
In cities and villages, beside the sea.
And the trains roll on, every day
Hundreds of people coming or going or running
away—
Goodbye, goodbye!
Into the forest's silence,
Outside the dark tunnel,
Out of the tunnel, out of the dark . . .

The Wind and the Rain

Like the wind, I run;
Like the rain, I sing;
Like the leaves, I dance;
Like the earth, I'm still;
And in this, Lord, I do thy will.

In This Workaday World

It's a busy world, I know,
And we must hurry here and there
And not ask who or why or where,
For fear our credits fall too low.
But here upon this hilly crest
There's some respite; and when
The fretting day is done,
Beneath the cherry tree there's rest.

To the Indian Foresters

You are the quiet men who do not boast
Although you've done much more than most
To make this land a sea of green
From here to far Cape Comorin.
Without your help to Nature's thrust,
This land would be a bowl of dust.
A land without its forest wealth
Must suffer a decline in health,
For herbs and plants all need green cover
Before they help the sick recover.
And we need trees to hold together
Beasts, and birds of every feather,
And leaves to help the air smell sweet;
And this and more is no mean feat.

Dear foresters, you have not sought for fame or favour,
Yours has been a love of labour.
Our thanks! Instead of desert sand
You've given us this green and growing land.

(Composed and read to a gathering of young forest officers at the Forest Research Institute on 10 April 2004)

We Rode All the Way to Delhi

In the Bicycle Age
When I was a kid
We rode all the way to Delhi,
Yes we did!
Somi and Ranji and I . . .
It took us three days
As we pressed on our pedals,
All two hundred miles
From Dehra to Delhi,
And they gave us no medals!
We sheltered in dhabas
And ate what they gave us,
 But no welcoming crowd
In Delhi received us
As dusty, dishevelled
We crossed the old bridge

And rode round the city
And camped on the Ridge.

Next day we rose late—
Our bodies they ached—
So instead of cycling
All the way back again
We put our bikes on the train
And went home in style
To Dehra from Delhi,
Somi and Ranji and I . . .

We Who Love Books

Some books I'll never give away,
Though old and worn, their binding torn,
Upon my shelves they'll always stay,
Alive, still read, still fresh each dawn,
Their magic moments never gone.

Great verse, great thoughts, still stand the test
Of time that's passing by so fast . . .
These good companions never fail
To give us joy, to nourish us . . .
We who love books will always be
The lucky ones,
Our minds set free.

My Best Friend

My best Friend
Is the baker's son,
I gave him a book
And he gave me a bun!

I told him a tale
Of a magical lake,
And he liked it so much
That he baked me a cake.

Yes, he's my best friend—
We go cycling together,
On bright sunny days,
Or in rain and bad weather.

And if we feel hungry
There's always a pie
Or a pastry to feast on,
As we go riding by!

Dare to Dream

Build castles in the air
But first, give them foundations.
Hold fast to all your dreams,
Make perfect your creations.

All glory comes to those who dare.

Failed works are sad lame things.
Act impeccably, sing
Your own song, but do not take
Another's song from her or him;
Look for your art within,
You'll find your own true gift,
For you are special too.
And if you try, you'll find
There's nothing you can't do.

And as We Part

The day is done,
It's time to sleep,
And with this world
To make my peace.
Enchanted days
Have all my life
Brought beauty
More than bitter strife.
May you who read
These words today
Be blessed in every way . . .
And as we part,
I give you all
That lies within my heart.